MOON CHOO-CHOO

A Tale of Imagination and Sibling Adventure

Story by **Mona Voelkel**   *Illustrated by* **Nancy Kincade**

For my husband, Ray, and our family:
You are my sun, my moon, and all my stars.
-E.E. Cummings
MV

For my family near and far.
NK

Everybody, time to play!
What should we pretend today?

Maybe we are engineers,
Fixing brakes and oiling gears.

Maybe we are astronauts,
Making suits from foil and pots.

Maybe we invent new things.
Take this train and give it wings.

Of course we need a flag to fly.
Draw a heart and hoist it high!

Moon Choo-Choo, Moon Choo-Choo,
Ready to fly?
Moon Choo-Choo, Moon Choo-Choo,
Reach for the sky!

Engine, Engine, Number 3,
Shooting through the galaxy.

Moon Choo-Choo, Moon Choo-Choo,
Ready to land!

Moon Choo-Choo, Moon Choo-Choo,
Hits crater sand....

We're flipping. We're floating.
We're dancing a tune.
We're laughing. We're smiling.
We're the kids on the moon.

Let's all have a lunar lunch,
Drink some Tang and munch, munch, munch.

Our engine fuel is running low.
Let's leave our flag and go, go, go!

Space explorers, hold on tight.
Touchdown's at the speed of flight.

After such a stellar day, it's hard to put our toys away.
But no matter what we do, it's always fun to be with you.

We've had a blast on Moon Choo-Choo!
Tomorrow we'll go somewhere new!

Mona Voelkel is "over the moon" to share this story inspired by the imaginative play of her three sons and two grandsons. This is her second collaboration with Nancy Kincade. Their first book together was *Stanley and the Wild Words*. A reading specialist, she lives in New York with her husband. Visit monavoelkel.com and follow her journey to encourage creativity, collaboration, and a love of words.

Nancy Kincade won a Christopher Award for *Even If I Did Something Awful*, one of several books she illustrated for Atheneum Books. After a very enjoyable career in art education, she is delighted to be illustrating once again. Her most recent books include *A God of Purpose: Fareena's Friendship* and *A God of Redemption: Hannah's Heartache*.

Text copyright © 2024 by Mona Voelkel
Illustrations copyright © 2024 by Nancy Kincade
All rights reserved. Copying or digitizing this book for storage, display, or distribution in any other medium is strictly prohibited.

For information about permission to reproduce selections from this book, please contact arignapress@icloud.com.
Visit www.monavoelkel.com for book news and resources.

ISBN: 978-1-7376955-4-7 (hc)
ISBN: 978-1-7376955-3-0 (pb)
ISBN: 978-1-7376955-5-4 (eBook)
Library of Congress Control Number: 2022901341

The text is set in Garamond with display type in Life Savers.
The illustrations are rendered in pencil and watercolor.

Made in the USA
Las Vegas, NV
04 April 2025